The Magical Mist

Elizabeth Monroy

Illustrated by Barbara Cate

Going Home Books

For more information please contact:
GOING HOME BOOKS
P.O. Box 688, Parker, AZ. 85344

First Printing 1995

Although the author and publisher have made every effort to ensure
the accuracy and completeness of information contained in this book,
we assume no responsibility for errors, inaccuracies, omissions, or any
inconsistency herein. Any slights of people, places, or organizations
are unintentional. For more information please contact: GOING
HOME BOOKS.

ISBN 0–9639760–0–1
Library of Congress Catalog Number: 93–091857

SUMMARY: Lauren's rag doll, Mirabelle, becomes magically alive and
leads her to the World of Imagination where she discovers that her
world is being consumed by a cloud of disbelief. Lauren must use the
magic key to the World of Imagination to free the Earth from the
chains of disbelief.

Published by: GOING HOME BOOKS
Book Design by Cheryl A. Kline
Edited by Toni Chavez

**ATTENTION SCHOOLS: ORGANIZATIONS,
& CHILDRENS' CENTERS**
Quantity discounts are available on bulk purchases of this book for
educational purposes or fund raising. Signature parties and
Empowering Your Child's Creativity workshops are also available by
the author.
Please contact: GOING HOME BOOKS,
P.O. Box 688, Parker, Az. 85344
or call 1 800 410–1999 fax 619 665–5565.

Dedicated to:
The Creative Imagination
within us all, large and small.

A Special Thanks to:
My husband, Peter, whose love, support,
and creative ideas made this book possible,
to my family, and all of my teachers
both seen and unseen,
especially Sharon and Patrick whose love
and teachings have made
the seemingly impossible, possible.

Once upon a time, not so very long ago there lived a little girl who had blond curls in her hair, green sparkles in her eyes, and red freckles on her nose. Her name was Lauren. Lauren's dearest and most loyal friend was Mirabelle, a stuffed rag doll. She had long, yellow, yarn braids and wore a pretty pink tutu with matching ballerina slippers. Lauren and Mirabelle did everything together.

Today, they were having a tea party under the shade of the great weeping willow tree. Lauren was just about to pour Mirabelle another cup of tea when she heard her mother call.
"Hurry Lauren, everyone's waiting for you to leave for the circus!" Lauren became so nervous she did something she'd never done before, she ran off forgetting all about pour Mirabelle who was left all alone at the tea table!

♦.♦.♦

hen Lauren reached her home at the top of the hill she found her family anxiously waiting. Everyone jumped into the car and drove off to see the circus. Everyone … that is … except Zeke, the Saint Bernard. He had to stay behind.

♦.♦.♦

The Great Cicero MAGIC SHOW

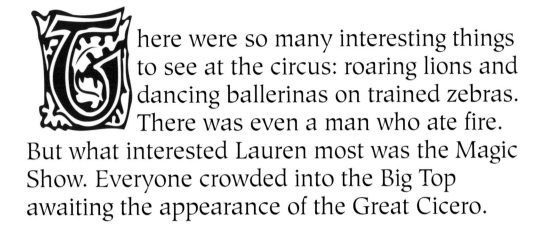here were so many interesting things to see at the circus: roaring lions and dancing ballerinas on trained zebras. There was even a man who ate fire. But what interested Lauren most was the Magic Show. Everyone crowded into the Big Top awaiting the appearance of the Great Cicero.

 puff of black smoke appeared in the center of the stage and out from the black billows walked the wizard. He had a pointy nose and a long gray beard. "Greetings! I am the Great Cicero, wise wizard and magician. You will witness here tonight feats that will out reach the farthest stretches of your imagination! Now let us begin."

A small boy was chosen from the audience, and a sheet was placed over him. With one wave of Cicero's magic wand the boy vanished! The Great Cicero waved his wand a second time, and the boy miraculously reappeared. Magic trick after magic trick Cicero marveled his audience.

♦.♦.♦

he time had come at last for the most spectacular feat of all. Lauren was chosen as the next volunteer, and the Great Cicero held up a very old and tarnished bottle.

"Inside this bottle are rainbows, moonbeams, mixed with a touch of star dust," he said gloating over his possession. "In here is the very fabric from which all dreams are woven! With just one drop of my Magical Mist anything is possible." He chuckled as he slowly unscrewed the cork. The people in the crowd held their breaths. Suddenly, a post from the Big Top gave way and came crashing down! Cicero dropped the magic bottle, and the strange mist oozed out.

♦.♦.♦

he Magical Mist hung mysteriously over the heads in the crowd, then it began to glow and change colors. The strange mist rose higher and higher until it disappeared right out of the hole in the center of the Big Top. "My mist, my Magical Mist," the Great Cicero moaned. "I'm finished without it!" he cried as he ran hopelessly after it.

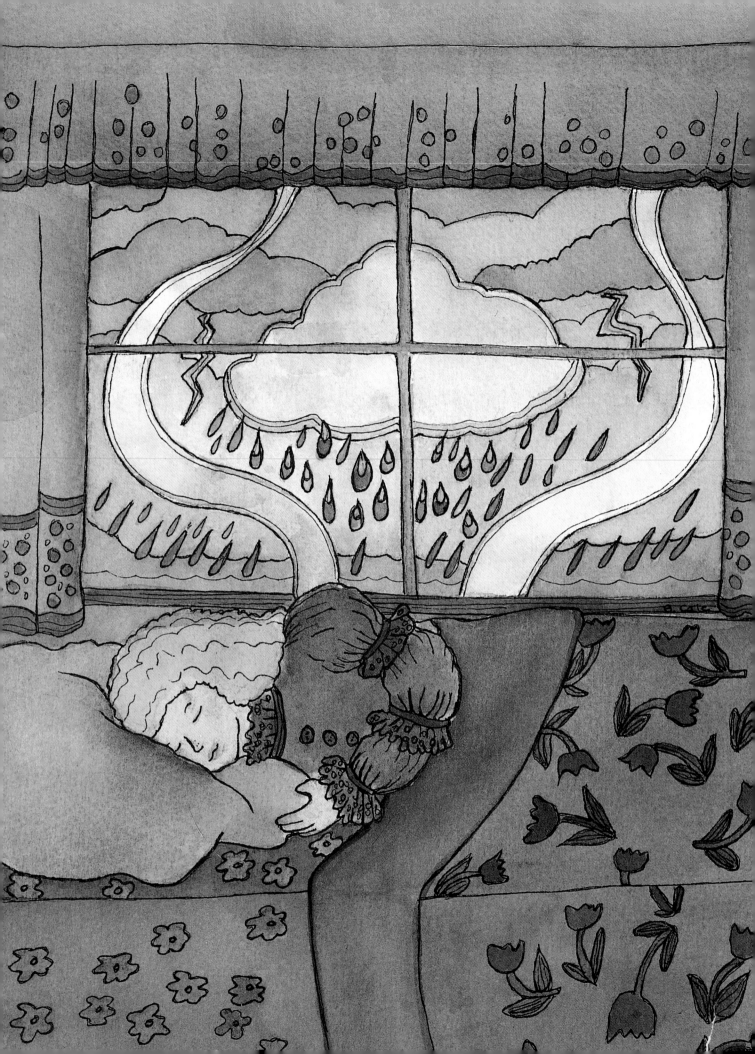

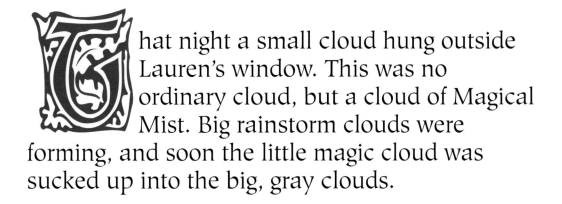

That night a small cloud hung outside Lauren's window. This was no ordinary cloud, but a cloud of Magical Mist. Big rainstorm clouds were forming, and soon the little magic cloud was sucked up into the big, gray clouds.

he wind blew fiercely and lightning flashed in the sky. The Magical Mist mixed with the raindrops, and a few of those magic raindrops found their way onto poor Mirabelle who, by this time, had fallen from her chair and lay on the wet, muddy ground. At that moment a wonderful thing occurred! Can you guess what happened?

Mirabelle became magically ALIVE!

he next day was bright and sunny. Lauren awoke from her dreams and looked around her room for Mirabelle, but she was no where to be found. She frantically looked about her house, but still no Mirabelle. She quickly dressed and ran out of the house with her mother calling after her. When she reached the weeping willow tree, she heard someone singing. She peered around the great trunk and there, to her amazement, was Mirabelle singing and dancing with Zeke! Lauren's mouth hung open and her eyes nearly popped right out of their sockets.

"Mirabelle! You're alive!" Lauren shouted as she picked up Mirabelle, hugging and kissing her.

Mirabelle and Lauren played together the whole day. They climbed trees, told stories, picked flowers, and had a real tea party! This time Mirabelle poured the tea. They were having so much fun they didn't realize it had grown quite late.

♦.♦.♦

auren burst into the house excited to surprise her family with the good news. But when Mirabelle looked into the stern, disbelieving eyes of Mrs. Allen, a strange thing happened. Her arms and legs became limp and her mouth froze into a painted grin.

"Where have you been all day Lauren?" Her mother glared down at her.

"Playing with Mirabelle, look Mother, she's alive!" Lauren held up the limp body of Mirabelle, which only dangled from her hand.

"I don't have time for your silly games. Upstairs, young lady, and don't come down until dinner!"

♦.♦.♦

auren realized that no one else could see the truth about Mirabelle, because everyone else had lost their imagination, everyone…that is… except Zeke.

But Lauren still believed in Mirabelle, even if no one else did.

When Lauren started school, Mirabelle waited patiently for her on the shelf and helped Lauren with her school work, because the Magical Mist had made Mirabelle a very wise doll.

t night Mirabelle and Lauren would fly up, up, up into the starry sky and turn somersaults beside the shimmering stars. One night Mirabelle set their course for the brightest star of all. It was so bright they had to shade their eyes with their hands as they entered the planet's atmosphere.

cheery Court Jester greeted them, then tooted his horn and a magnificent King and Queen appeared. "I am King Infinite and this is my Queen Fantasia. We have been waiting for you."

"You are our only hope, my child," the Queen sighed," a cloud of disbelief has cast its shadow on your world, it grows thicker and thicker every day. If something is not done all imagination will be lost from your world forever."

"But what can I do?" Lauren asked.

"I think I may have a plan, but first let's celebrate, it isn't every day a child finds their way to our Planet."

Lauren and Mirabelle were crowned Princesses and escorted to a magnificent banquet in the most splendid of palaces. The ceiling stretched into the stars, and the walls were made of crystals which changed colors when you touched them. Mirabelle thought of blue and the wall became a pale blue, Lauren thought of pink and the crystals changed into an icy pink. In the center of the great hall was a large table filled with strange food: blue grapes, orange bananas, and green mashed potatoes! A roly–poly man with a green face, and blue hair held up a jar of jelly.

"Try some of my jolly jelly," he laughed,"it makes everything you spread it on funny!"

"No. No, have a bite of my light, and airy purple pudding," pleaded a checkerboard knight. Lauren and Mirabelle took a spoonful of each and began giggling, then they floated right out of their seats.

◆ . ◆ . ◆

usic!" cried the Queen and a band of crickets appeared, followed by a symphony of hummingbirds, and an orchestra of violins.

"How do we get down?"Lauren giggled.

"Just think yourself down," roared the King. "That's how everything works here, you think and it happens." BOOM! Lauren and Mirabelle landed in their seats with a thud. When a polka dotted Princess offered Lauren a piece of hiccup cake, she politely declined.

"What a shame if all this was lost from the Earth forever, "Lauren thought to herself. The Queen clapped her hands and the Jester appeared with a beautiful golden key. "The Key to the World of Imagination!" the Queen announced. Then she bent down and gently whispered into Lauren's ear," If used at the proper moment, with the correct intent, this key could release your world from the chains of disbelief forever! Stay true to yourself my dear, there will be those who will try and stop you, but you must stay out from under the cloud of disbelief. Your entire World depends on it." She kissed Lauren on the cheek. Lauren placed the key around Mirabelle's neck for safe keeping, and they flew home.

he next day Mrs. Grundy, Lauren's school teacher, met with Lauren's parents. "Mr. and Mrs. Allen," Mrs. Grundy snorted as she peered over her horn rimmed glasses, "your daughter is a very bright little girl, however, she is a disruption to the discipline and order of my classroom. She finishes all her assignments early and insists on distracting the other students with ridiculous stories about talking rag dolls, magic keys, and worlds of imagination. Such impracticalities simply won't be tolerated! Now, I am a patient woman, but I'm afraid if we don't do something about this behavior soon, others won't be so understanding."

"I don't know what to do with her, Mrs. Grundy," Mrs. Allen sighed.

"Leave it to me, Mrs. Allen. I'll see to it she doesn't have time for such frivolous activities!" And Mrs. Grundy smiled a sour grin.

♦.♦.♦

hat afternoon Mirabelle waited patiently for Lauren to come home. She waited and waited.

Finally, as the moon rose in the autumn sky, Lauren rushed into the room, set down a large stack of books and rushed out again. Mirabelle called to her from the shelf, but the door had already slammed shut. Late that night a very tired Lauren crawled into bed. "Let's go on a magical adventure!" Mirabelle shouted as she jumped onto Lauren's pillow. But Lauren only rolled over in her sleep crushing poor Mirabelle who laid there all night scarcely able to breathe.

he next morning Lauren was in such a hurry to get to school she didn't even notice Mirabelle tangled in the bed sheets. Lauren became much too busy to think about Mirabelle or the World of Imagination. Despite Mirabelle's efforts, the cloud of disbelief was swallowing Lauren up. Without Lauren to love her or believe in her, Mirabelle grew weaker and weaker until she could not move at all.

One day while Mrs. Allen was tiding up Lauren's room, she came across Mirabelle's lifeless body. "I think Lauren has finally outgrown this dusty old thing." And she pitched poor Mirabelle right into the garbage can.

♦.♦.♦

irabelle lay helplessly on top of the garbage heap with the golden key to the World of Imagination dangling from her neck. "How will Lauren save our World if she doesn't even have the magic key?" Mirabelle thought of a World with no imagination as she watched the evening stars come out. "No more dreams, or hopes, only despair." A tear trickled down her painted face. In the morning, the garbage men would come and take her away, and she would never see Lauren again.

Just then, Mirabelle felt a cold nose brush against her. It was Zeke! He'd come to rescue her. Zeke gently pulled her from the garbage and carried her to the weeping willow tree where he hid Mirabelle with his favorite bone.

◆.◆.◆

hile Mirabelle slumbered, Lauren grew up. She forgot all about Mirabelle and the World of Imagination as the cloud of disbelief shadowed her more each day. As the cloud grew thicker and thicker around the Earth's atmosphere, more and more people became filled with despair. Imagination was about to be lost from the World forever! But there was one little girl who had managed so far, to escape the deadly cloud of disbelief. Her name was April, and she was Lauren's daughter.

One day while April and Lauren were visiting April's grandmother, April went outside to play with Zeke. When they came to the weeping willow tree, Zeke started digging and uncovered Mirabelle. April was so excited to see such a beautiful rag doll she hugged and kissed Mirabelle. April's love opened Mirabelle's sleepy eyes and once again she could move and talk. April was thrilled to see a rag doll that was really alive! They sang, danced, and went for a long walk in the woods.

◆.◆.◆

irabelle told April about the cloud of disbelief, and the magic key that could unlock the chains of disbelief if used at the correct moment. April thought and thought, and finally decided to show her mother the key. Maybe she would remember how to use it. As Mirabelle and April hurried home, April tripped and fell into a steep ravine. She struggled to climb out, but the earth gave way. She grabbed hold of a small branch, and held on for dear life.

♦.♦.♦

eke and Mirabelle ran for help. Mrs. Allen heard Zeke's barking and opened the door. "I thought I threw this old thing out years ago," Mrs. Allen grumbled as she picked up Mirabelle and started toward the garbage. "Wait!" cried Lauren, and she pulled Mirabelle from her mother's grip. As Lauren held Mirabelle, she stared at the magic key dangling from her neck. The key began to glow, and a spark of imagination leapt from the key right into Lauren's mind. Mirabelle concentrated on April hanging over the ravine and Lauren was able to see April's predicament. "April! She's in trouble!" Lauren cried and ran to save her daughter.

◆.◆.◆

pril was barely holding on by the time her mother arrived. Lauren swung herself over the ledge and held her hand out, but April could not reach it. Lauren stretched and stretched, but she still could not reach her daughter whose grip was weakening by the moment.

Mirabelle grabbed the magic key which hung around her neck. "Lauren, use the key to the World of Imagination!"

Lauren, whose heart was filled with love for her daughter, took hold of the magic key. She squeezed it tightly and whispered, "I believe in your infinite power." The key began to glow. As Lauren stretched the key toward her daughter, a strange mist enveloped them both, and April felt herself being lifted up into the safety of her mother's arms.

♦.♦.♦

rs. Allen arrived out of breath. "How did you ever know to look for April here?" "Mirabelle told her, Gramma!" April smiled. Mirabelle looked up into Mrs. Allen's face and noticed tears filling her eyes. One of them streamed down her face and washed away all the years of harshness and disbelief. As Mrs. Allen's eyes softened, she could see that Mirabelle really was alive. At that very same moment the cloud of disbelief lifted its shadow from the planet Earth and vanished forever!

The Queen smiled down from her throne in the World of Imagination, and her voice thundered forth, "You have used the key wisely Lauren and saved your World!" From that day on the people of planet Earth were free to dream, imagine, and create. Mirabelle, April, Lauren, and Gramma told stories, picked flowers, had tea parties, and went on magical adventures to the World of Imagination!

*… and they all lived magically
ever after!*

THE END